W9-BOO-942

Charles M. Schulz

My Best Friend, My Blanket

HarperHorizon
An Imprint of HarperCollinsPublishers 120030

First published in 1998 by HarperCollins*Publishers* Inc.
http://www.harpercollins.com
Copyright © 1998 United Feature Syndicate, Inc. All rights reserved.
HarperCollins ® and ▲ ® are trademarks of HarperCollins*Publishers* Inc. PEANUTS is a registered trademark of United Feature Syndicate, Inc.
PEANUTS © United Feature Syndicate, Inc. Based on the PEANUTS ® comic strip by Charles M. Schulz
http://www.unitedmedia.com
ISBN 0-694-01044-8
Printed in Canada.

"Notice anything?"

"Like what?"

"My blanket is gone! I've given it up!
I don't need it anymore!"

"When did this happen?"

"Four minutes ago."

"I want to write a book. I want to tell everyone how I gave up my blanket."

"Maybe you can think of a good title, Snoopy . . ."

"What I think I'll do is go from house to house telling people how I gave up my blanket. I'll knock on every door! I'll help all the little kids in the world who can't give up their blankets."

"Your head doesn't even feel warm!"

"Good morning, little girl. You sure are a cute little thing. I see you have a security blanket."

"Would you like to have me tell you how I broke myself of that habit?"

"Stupid kid!"

"I ran an ad in the paper for my clinic."

"Your clinic?"

"I'm going to teach little kids how to give up their blankets! Hundreds of kids will come knocking on my door!"

KNOCK
KNOCK
KNOCK
KNOCK

"Hi, my name is Linus. I take it you've come here to learn how to give up your blanket."

"My folks made me come."

"You say your name is Randolph? Let's get to work. I'm going to help you to give up your blanket. First, however, I have to ask you a few personal questions."

"May I ask why you wear your blanket over your head?"

"So you won't see the three teddy bears I'm holding!"

"Before we continue with your treatment, we need to do something. I'm going to ask you to take the blanket off your head."

"Anything you say..."

"Aaugh!"

"I could have given up this blanket."

"But I was driven back to it
by treachery!"